First published in 2004

Allen & Unwin
83 Alexander St
Crows Nest NSW 2065
Australia
Phone: (61 2) 8425 0100
Fax: (61 2) 9906 2218
Email: info@allenandunwin.com
Web: www.allenandunwin.com

National Library of Australia
Cataloguing-in-Publication entry:
Fienberg, Anna.
There once was a boy called Tashi.
ISBN 1 74114 198 2.
1. Tashi (Fictitious character) – Juvenile fiction.
I. Gamble, Kim. II. Fienberg, Barbara. III. Title.
A823.3

Kim Gamble used watercolours for the artwork in this book.

Cover and text design by Sandra Nobes
Set in Old Claude by Tou-Can Design
Printed in China by Everbest Printing Co. Ltd.

3 5 7 9 10 8 6 4 2

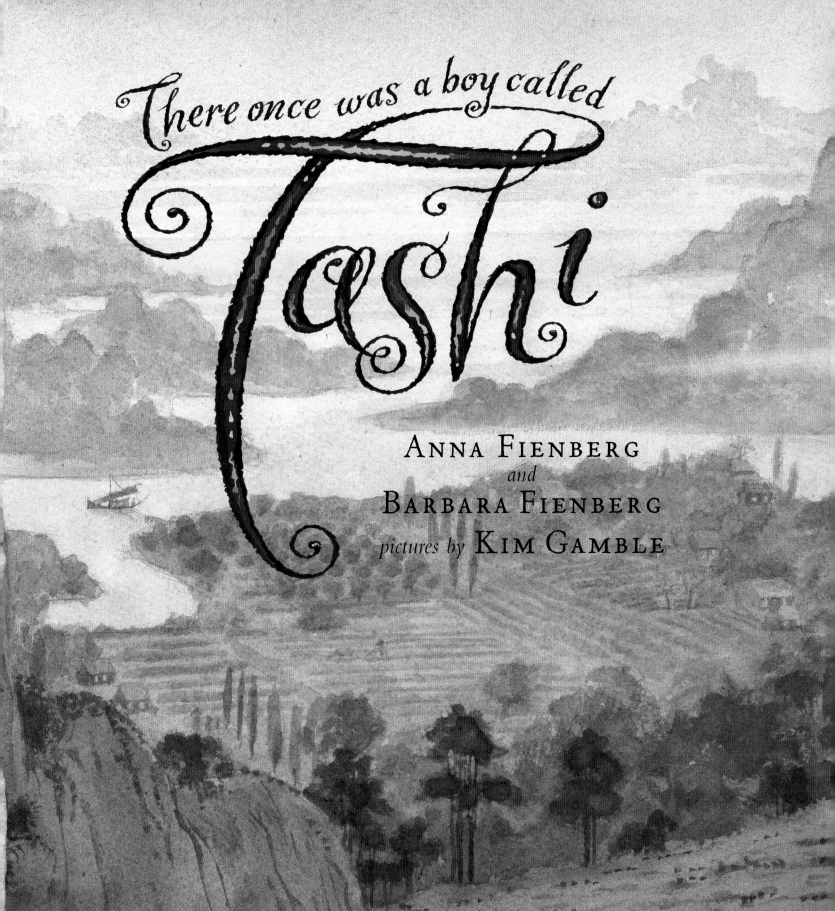

There once was a boy called Tashi

ANNA FIENBERG
and
BARBARA FIENBERG
pictures by KIM GAMBLE

There once was a boy called Tashi,
who had a way with witches and warlords and guessed
the secrets of ghosts. His grandmother knew where
dragons dwelled and Luk Ahed told him the future.
He listened to Wise-as-an-Owl read magic from
the Book of Spells, and Second Uncle
showed him how to follow the stars.

Tashi wasn't afraid of the
giant on the mountain

or the wicked Baron by the river,
but never, *ever*, had he dreamed
of an ogre such as Gloomin.

From high on the hill,
Tashi was the first to see the ogre.
The Magic Warning Bell
screamed out from
the village – so loud it
seemed the *sky* would break –

but still Gloomin came, his great boots slamming
into the earth like doors on the giant's castle.

People hurried into their houses and closed the shutters.
But Tashi ran down the hill and into the square. He felt
the ground tremble beneath his feet. He saw the sky grow
dark. And when the ogre Gloomin strode into the village,
Tashi heard his mournful song:

Black and cold and bitter as brine,
That's my heart since I lost what's mine.

Gloomin trampled gardens.
He picked up dustbins and
scrabbled through them.

He searched under bushes,
dug through pot plants,
flung about people's washing.

And then,
he took off the roof of Hai Ping's house,
just like that, and sat down in it.

Tashi wanted to ask the ogre what it was that he'd lost,
but the pool of darkness that followed
Gloomin's feet made him silent.

Dark seeped out of Hai Ping's house,
spilling onto the path, across the square.
Ghosts drifted in, hiding in the damp folds of
people's curtains, mooning about in their rice bowls.
And winter settled over the village.

At Tashi's house, Grandma had to light the
lamps at breakfast and keep a fire roaring
in the hearth all day.

'The Gloomin winter,' Luk Ahed, the fortune teller, called it,
writing in his charts. Luk Ahed said *he'd* seen something
dark moving towards them weeks before,
but he'd thought it was just rain.

Tashi watched Grandma's tomatoes wither
with frost, her carrots shrivel into the earth.

'Will we have winter for *all* our lives?'
his cousin Lotus Blossom asked him.

Gloomin stole chickens from Second Uncle and a pig from Third Aunt. But when he began to eye *people* for his cooking pot, Tashi knew he would have to do something about Gloomin.

That dark morning Tashi went to visit Wise-as-an-Owl. The old man opened his Book of Spells, and sighed. 'I'm sorry, Tashi, the Book only tells me this: Ogres of these parts have one hundred and four teeth, they eat people, and they keep a pet, called a *familiar*, to share their fireside and household chores.'

Tashi thanked Wise-as-an-Owl and went to see Luk Ahead.
When the fortune teller opened his charts of the stars, he sighed.
'I'm sorry, Tashi, the charts only tell me this: Ogres of these parts
are famous for their dark moods, called the *melancholy*,
and when they are especially sad, ogres have been
known to cause years of winter.'

Tashi thanked Luk Ahed and walked slowly away.
An idea was forming in his head.

'Where are you going?'
asked Lotus Blossom.

'Into the forest,' said Tashi.
'I'm looking for a *familiar*
to mend a *melancholy*.'

'A what for a what?
Well if you are going into the forest
you'll have to cross the bridge by the wicked Baron's house.
And you know that's risky. I'll come too.'

So Tashi and Lotus Blossom set off through the fields.
They searched through the long grass as they went.
They looked through hedges
and down foxholes.

'Do you belong to Gloomin?'
Tashi asked a young rabbit
diving into her burrow.
The rabbit just blinked
at him and disappeared.

'Do you belong to Gloomin?'
Tashi woke a bear cub
snoozing in a cave.
'Grrizznff,' growled the bear,
and went back to sleep.

Lotus Blossom climbed a tree
but all she found was a baby
ghost hiding in the branches.

They were just stepping off the bridge
when they saw the wicked Baron. He was
sneaking along the path, and in his arms he was
holding a sack as carefully as if it were a pot of gold.

And from the sack there came a high thin voice:

Greedy and mean and sly as a snake,
The Baron did catch me, oh what a mistake!

Tashi ran up to him and blocked
his path. 'Oh Baron, I see you have a fine new
cat in that sack. I'm looking for such a cat as that.'
The Baron roughly pushed the cat's head down into the sack.

'You can't have this one, young Tashi. This is a very special cat.'

'You won't sell it for any price?'

'Not for any you could pay,' spat the Baron, and tried to push past.

Tashi stood his ground.
'Perhaps we could strike a bargain.
Yesterday Wise-as-an-Owl
let me read a page of his
Book of Spells.'

'So?' snorted the Baron.

Tashi looked about and picked up an old iron horseshoe
lying in the grass. He dangled it on his finger.
'I learned how to turn iron such as this into gold.'

The Baron's eyes glistened.
'Don't tell me you can really turn rusty metal into gold?'

Tashi nodded. 'Give me the cat and I'll tell you.'

The Baron thrust the sack into Tashi's arms and Tashi said,
'It's very simple. Just lay the horseshoe in this pool of water and
say these words.' He whispered the spell into the Baron's ear.

Tashi and Lotus Blossom left the Baron
crouched over the horseshoe, whispering and waiting.

'Will it turn into gold, Tashi?'
Lotus Blossom worried as they went.

'Maybe,' Tashi said airily.
'I didn't have time to read the whole page.'

And so Tashi and Lotus Blossom crossed back over the bridge,
past the ghost in the tree and the bear cub snoozing. When they
neared the village they began to run and Tashi's heart felt light,
as if it could float up and lift him from the ground.

At the gate of Hai Ping's house,
the cat jumped out of the bag and rubbed against Tashi's legs.

Gloomin came bursting out of the house like a wild wind.

Cat! You ran off without warning,
And left me here, sick with mourning.
You didn't say why, just dashed away,
Full of the fish I'd caught that day.

The cat purred and leapt into Gloomin's arms.
She nuzzled close and said:

Now you can see how busy I've been.
Here are two kittens, fit for a queen.

Gloomin bent down. He stroked the little kittens. Then he smiled
so broadly that all one hundred and four teeth showed.

Let's go home now, Gloomin, my dear.
You'll care for us better there than here.

So Tashi and Lotus Blossom watched the great ogre
pick up his family of cats and stride off happily into the forest,
back the way he'd come. And as they watched,
they saw the dark dry up like puddles after a summer storm.

The next day a grand feast was held in the square
and the villagers thanked Tashi, dancing while the flowers bloomed.

'I knew you would think of something, Tashi, my love,'
Grandma said, and the sun spread across her knees like a warm rug.